# Dumped

# Dumped

written and illustrated
by Britton Payne

BLOOMSBURY

Published by Bloomsbury, New York and London
Distributed to the trade by Holtzbrinck Publishers

Cataloging-in-Publication Data is available from the Library of Congress

ISBN 1-58234-331-4

First U.S. Edition 2003

10  9  8  7  6  5  4  3  2  1

Printed and bound by C&C Offset Printing Co., Hong Kong

You got
dumped

by the person who knew
you best

knew you
better than
anyone else

who got to know
the real you

and decided
not to stick around

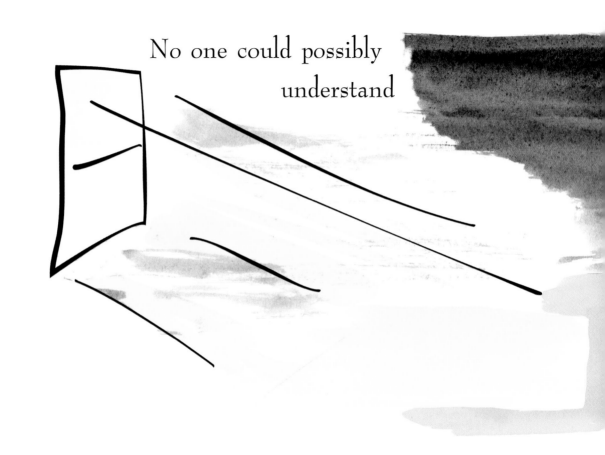

how you feel

You hate yourself
for loving the one
you hate

You hate yourself for hating the one you love

No one else could ever love you that much

No one will ever love you again

Now you have to tell her you're alone

which is almost as bad as being alone

which you are

You ache

You're boring your friends

singing along
with sad songs

loudly

running out of Kleenex

and ice cream

You can't see beyond this

but

maybe it
wasn't
meant
to last

and maybe it wasn't
really what you'd
hoped it was, anyway

There are a million great people out there

so go to the park

make something

throw some stuff away

let your mind move on to other things

and seriously, don't call

Remember

everybody has had their heart broken

even your mother

You'll find someone who loves you

the way your ex never did

You'll get your happy ending

To Tara, my happy ending

Thanks to Sarah Burnes, whose extraordinary guidance and contributions extended well above and beyond what I ever would have expected of an agent, with whom I gladly share any credit for your enjoyment of this book, to Colin Dickerman and Karen Rinaldi for their guidance and faith in my vision, to Andrea Lynch for her generous contributions to the book and its presentation, Susan Burns, Greg Villepique and all the talented and dedicated people at Bloomsbury, Julina Tatlock for her belief in me and for connecting me with Sarah, Bill Clegg for starting an agency with Sarah that would take on a project like this, and my wonderful and incredible mom, Dale Longstreth, my hero. I also offer special thanks for the inspiration and support from Joan Higgins, Penny Payne, Chris Kalb, Eli Cooper, Gary Greenberg, Jack Lambert, Dick Grayson, Tara's terrific family, my dad, my brother, my fantastic family, and Jake.